STORY BY
Lesléa Newman

PICTURES BY
Amy June Bates

Gittel's Journey

AN ELLIS ISLAND STORY

Abrams Books for Young Readers · NEW YORK

"Gittel, will you write to me from America?" Raisa asked.

"Yes," Gittel answered, "and you can write back and tell me how Frieda likes living with you." Gittel turned to Mama, who was standing in the doorway, wiping one of her eyes with the worn white handkerchief she always kept in her pocket. "Can't we take Frieda with us?" she asked for the hundredth time.

"No, Gittel," Mama replied, also for the hundredth time. "We cannot bring a goat to America. Now come inside and set the table. The sun is about to set, and it's time to light the candles for *Shabbos*."

M ama lit the tall, white candles, and she and Gittel circled
their hands three times to gather in the Sabbath light.

Together they sang the blessing and then sat
down to eat.

The next morning, Gittel pulled on a heavy woolen skirt and sweater, two pairs of socks, and her winter coat and boots. Mama handed her a sack that held two apples, a large hunk of bread, and a small wedge of cheese.

"Farewell, Raisa. *Zei gezunt*." Gittel kissed Raisa on the cheek and then hugged Raisa's mama, papa, and baby brother. "*Zei gezunt*, Frieda." Gittel gave the little white goat one last pat on the head and then turned away. Mama had told Gittel that she had to be very brave, so she blinked her eyes and tried not to cry. Mama blinked her eyes, too, and dabbed at them with her handkerchief. Then she and Gittel started off.

"Wait, Gittel," Raisa called. "Basha wants to come with you." Raisa held out the rag doll she and Gittel loved to play with. Gittel looked at Mama, who had made her leave her own rag doll and so many other things behind.

"It's all right, Gittel." Mama blinked and wiped her eye again. "Say thank you to Raisa."

"A *sheynem dank*," Gittel said, as she tucked the small doll into her coat pocket. And then she and Mama set off on their long walk to the port.

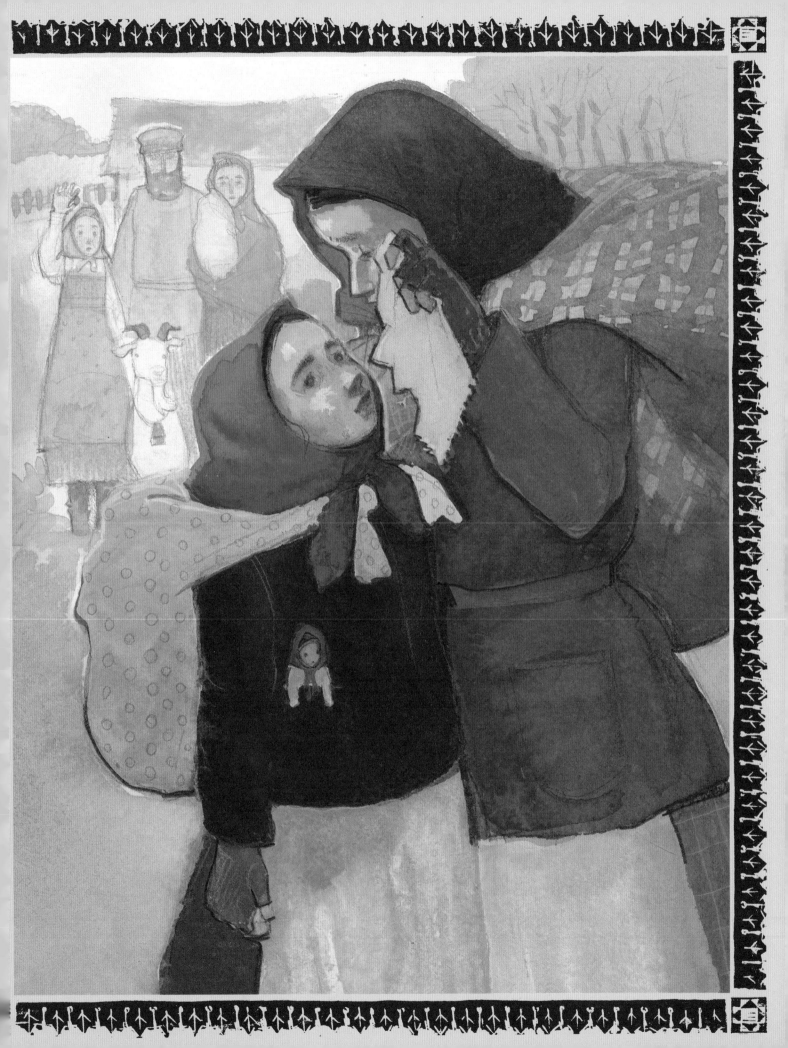

Many other people were making their way toward the seacoast. Some were on foot, some sat on donkeys, and a few rode in horse-drawn carts.

When Gittel and her mother arrived at the port, they entered a big building and stepped into line. "Stay close to me," Mama said, taking Gittel's hand, "and do just as I tell you."

"I will, Mama," Gittel said. There were many people jostling about, and one of them pushed

Gittel right up against her mother's soft woolen coat. It tickled her nose, and she sneezed loudly.

"Gittel!" her mother hissed. "No sneezing."

"Why?" Gittel asked. What was wrong with sneezing?

Mama gave Gittel a stern look. "You must be quiet as a mouse," Mama whispered, "and not draw attention to yourself."

Soon Gittel and her mother reached the head of the line. "Stick out your tongue," a burly man with a bristly beard ordered Gittel. "Blink your eyes. Show me your hands." Gittel did as she was told. The man nodded and then turned to Mama. "What is wrong with your eye?"

"It's nothing," said Mama. "I shed a few tears over leaving my home. Surely you can understand that."

"I understand all right," the man said. "Dry your eye and come back to me." The man turned to the next person in line while Mama wiped her runny eye. Then she returned to the man.

"Your eye is still red. It is an infection. Your request to go to America is denied."

"But—"

"Next!" The man turned his back.

Mama pulled at the man's sleeve. "Sir," she pleaded.

"Go home." The man brushed Mama's hand off his sleeve like a crumb of *challah*. "Next!"

"Come, Mama, let's go home," said Gittel, smiling at the thought. "Won't Raisa and Frieda be surprised?"

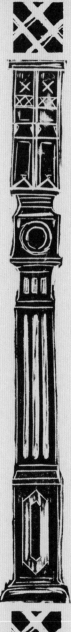

Gittel," Mama put her hands on Gittel's shoulders and looked her in the eye. "Home is not safe for us. You are going to America to have a better life."

"By myself?" Gittel's voice came out in a squeak. She was only nine years old. How could she go to America without Mama?

"You must be very brave, Gittel. Take this." Mama handed her a small cloth bundle. "My *Shabbos* candlesticks are wrapped inside. Be careful not to lose them. And here is your ticket. And this," Mama handed Gittel a folded piece of paper. "This is my cousin's name and address. Do not lose this paper. When you get to America, show it to an immigration officer. He will help you find my cousin. Mendel is expecting us. He will welcome you."

"But Mama—"

"*Shah, shayneh maidel*. No crying." Mama held up a finger. "Do you want your eye to get infected like mine? Then you won't be able to go either."

"I don't want to go. I want to stay here with you."

"*Shah*," Mama said again, folding Gittel's hand around the piece of paper. "This is God's plan. God will take care of you."

Gittel stepped into line. The ship was so big, it made Gittel feel very, very small. An officer took her ticket, pinned an identification tag onto her coat, and waved her on board. Gittel scurried up a steep staircase and pushed her way to the front of the crowd. She grabbed on to the ship's cold, wet railing with one hand, and, with the other tightly clenching the paper, she waved until the ship pulled away from the dock and Mama was out of sight.

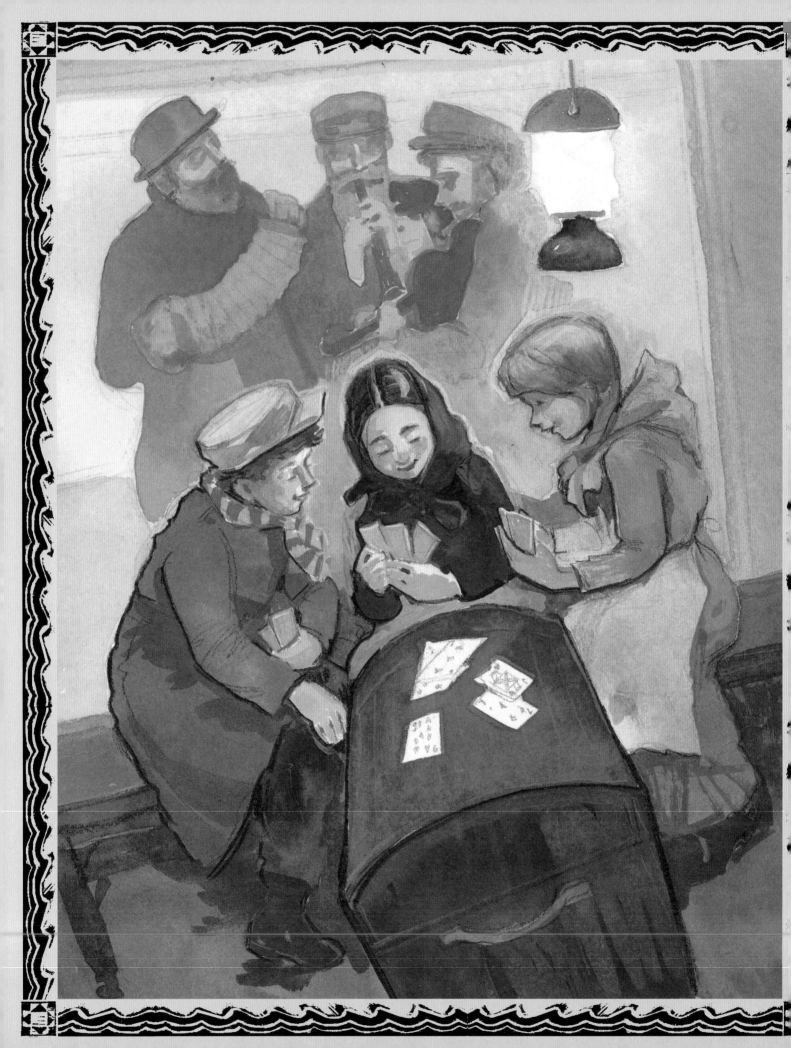

Gittel held on to the piece of paper with the name and address of Mama's cousin, just as Mama had told her to. She gripped it tightly while she stood in line with her dinner pail, and she carefully placed it on her lap as she sat down on a hard wooden bench to eat her herring and soup.

"Come play cards with my brother and me," a Yiddish-speaking girl called to Gittel. She pushed the piece of paper down into her skirt pocket and went to join their game. Later, she made sure the paper was still safely tucked away as she clapped along to a lively tune some jolly men were singing, even though she didn't understand a word.

Gittel spent many lonely hours sitting on her berth, talking to Basha. "I miss Raisa," she said to the little rag doll. "I miss Frieda. I miss Mama," Gittel wailed. When *Shabbos* arrived, Gittel cried an ocean of tears. She had Mama's candlesticks but no candles. Mama had candles but no candlesticks. Candles and candlesticks belonged together just as she and Mama belonged together. Gittel shut her eyes and sang the Sabbath blessing softly to herself. It only made her sadder.

The journey continued, and Gittel continued holding on to her piece of paper. She slid it under her pillow at night as she lay on her scratchy straw mattress, longing for Mama to sing her a lullaby. And she squeezed it during the day as she sat on her metal berth, worrying about her new life in America. "What if Mama's cousin Mendel doesn't like me?" Gittel asked Basha. "What if my new teacher doesn't like me? What if English is too hard to learn? What if I never see Mama again?" Gittel stared into Basha's shiny, black button eyes looking for answers, but Basha had no reply.

One morning, there was a big commotion on the boat. Gittel scrambled up on deck to see what all the excitement was about. "Look, look." Everyone pointed in the same direction as a great cheer arose. "There she is."

"Who?" Gittel asked.

"The Statue of Liberty," said a man standing beside Gittel, as he waved his cap in the air and wept. "She's welcoming us to America."

Gittel looked across the water and gasped at the sight of an enormous woman rising out of the ocean, wearing a crown and holding a torch high in the air. She was the most astonishing thing that Gittel had ever seen, and she wished Mama were standing beside her so she could see the enormous woman, too.

Soon the ship pulled into the harbor, and its loud, shrill whistle blew. Gittel placed Basha inside her coat pocket, next to her note from Mama, and rushed down the gangplank with all the other passengers. Their boots and shoes made quite a clatter! Gittel stepped off the ship, happy to feel solid ground beneath her feet for the first time in two weeks. Soon she found herself on board another boat, a small, crowded barge heading for Ellis Island. Cold ocean spray smacked Gittel in the face, and when she licked her lips, she tasted salt. But she didn't mind. Any minute now, she would be in America!

When the barge docked, Gittel got off the ship and joined a crowd trudging up a steep stairway into a giant room filled with so many people speaking so loudly in so many languages that Gittel couldn't understand a thing. At the top of the stairs, a doctor hastily looked her over and quickly waved her through.

Gittel waited in a long line until finally she stood before a man wearing thick glasses. He sat on a tall chair, scowling down at her and barking sharp, unfamiliar words. She wanted to run away, but Mama had told her to be brave, so she took a deep breath and stayed where she was. The man shouted again, and then another man stepped over, glanced at the identification tag pinned to her coat, and spoke.

"*Vi heystu?*" asked the man.

Hearing the familiar Yiddish words made Gittel feel a little less afraid. "*Ikh heys Gittel,*" she replied. "Please take me to my mama's cousin." She handed the interpreter the piece of paper Mama had given her back home. "His name is Mendel. Here is his address."

The interpreter unfolded the paper and looked at it. He turned it over. Then he turned it back. "There is no address here," he said to Gittel in a gentle voice.

"Yes, there is," Gittel said. "My mama wrote it down for me."

"See for yourself," said the interpreter. Gittel looked at the piece of paper. There was nothing on it but a fat blue smear.

The immigration officer wearing thick glasses pointed to Gittel's hand, which was spotted with ink, and muttered something to the interpreter. "What is this Mendel's last name?" the interpreter asked.

"I don't know," Gittel answered. "What will I do?" Tears spilled from her eyes.

"*Shah*," said the interpreter. "Don't cry. We will take care of you."

Gittel stayed where she was while the kind interpreter spoke to one immigrant after another in many different languages. When Gittel grew tired, the interpreter pulled out a chair so she could sit next to the scowling immigration officer. When Gittel grew hungry, the interpreter gave her a bowl of soup. And when Gittel grew bored, the interpreter whisked the immigration officer's cap off his head and placed it on Gittel's with a laugh.

"Say, that would make a swell picture," said a man with a large camera who snapped Gittel's photo.

"That gives me an idea," the interpreter said.

That night, Gittel lay on a thin mattress in a dormitory on Ellis Island, surrounded by strangers.

She had no pillow, so she put her lumpy cloth bundle under
her head, clutched Basha tightly, and cried herself to sleep.

The next day, the interpreter came to find her. He had a big smile on his face and a folded Jewish newspaper tucked under his arm.

"Do you recognize this *shayneh maidel?*" he asked Gittel, pointing to the paper.

"It's me!" Gittel cried, amazed to see her photo on the very front page.

That afternoon, the interpreter brought a man to see her. It was Mama's cousin Mendel come to take her home. "I saw you in the paper and recognized you right away," Mendel said to her. "You look just like your mama."

Uncle Mendel sent Mama the newspaper so she could see how famous Gittel had become. He helped Gittel write a letter to Raisa, too.

Months passed before Gittel received a letter back from Mama. "My eye is all healed," Mama wrote. "I will see you soon." And a few weeks later, she stepped through the gates of Ellis Island to gather Gittel into her arms.

"Come, Mama." Gittel kissed Mama's cheek, stepped back, and took her by the hand. "Let's go home. The sun is about to set, and it's time to light the candles for *Shabbos*."

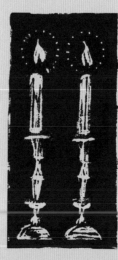

AUTHOR'S NOTE

Gittel's Journey is based on a true story.

Actually, *Gittel's Journey* is based on two true stories from my childhood. The first story was told to me by my grandmother Ruth Levin ("Grandma Ruthie"), who grew up in what she always called the "Old Country."

"Sometimes it was Russia, sometimes it was Poland." My grandmother would shrug. "The borders were always changing." Ruth, who was called by her Yiddish name Rukhl, was born in 1890 and lived with her mother and father. Her nine siblings were much older than she was, and all of them had immigrated to America by the late 1800s. When Rukhl's father died, she and her mother (my great-grandmother) also decided to immigrate. The year was 1900, and my grandmother was ten years old.

When my grandmother and great-grandmother got to Ellis Island, they weren't allowed to leave because it was forbidden for two females to enter America alone. They spent the night on the island in a dormitory until the next day when one of my grandmother's older brothers came to claim them.

They had brought very little to America, but one thing my great-grandmother did carry over was her set of brass *Shabbos* candlesticks, which were later handed down to my grandmother. In 1989, when she was ninety-nine years old, my Grandma Ruthie gave these candlesticks to me. I always think of her on Friday nights when I light the *Shabbos* candles.

THE AUTHOR AND GRANDMA RUTHIE (RUTH LEVIN) IN 1989.
PHOTO BY SUE TYLER.

The second story was told to me by my "aunt" Phyllis, who met my mother when they were both ten years old and who became her best friend. Aunt Phyllis's mother, Sadie Gringrass, was one of eight children who also grew up in the Old Country. Since her eldest sibling was married and had already started a family, their parents decided to send thirteen-year-old Sadie, the second oldest, to America to have "a better life." In 1911, Sadie began her journey with an aunt. But when they arrived at the port, her aunt was not allowed onto the ship leaving for America because of an eye infection.

THE AUTHOR AND AUNT PHYLLIS IN 2016. PHOTO BY MARY VAZQUEZ.

Sadie continued the trip by herself, traveling across the ocean alone. Her aunt had given her a piece of paper with the name and address of a relative on it. Sadie held the paper so tightly during the voyage that all the ink wore off on her hand. Her photo was placed in a Jewish newspaper, and that's how her relatives found her. Sadie worked and saved enough money to bring one of her younger sisters to America, but she never saw her mother and father again.

These are only two of the millions of stories of immigrants coming to America through Ellis Island between 1892 and 1954, including those of many children, some younger than Gittel and others older. In fact, the very first person to enter the United States through Ellis Island was a teenage girl named Annie Moore, who arrived from County Cork, Ireland, on

January 1, 1892. She was given a ten-dollar gold coin as a reward for being the very first immigrant to register at Ellis Island.

When steamships arrived from Europe, first- and second-class passengers were examined briefly while still on board the ship and then given landing cards, which allowed them to enter America. Passengers who traveled in steerage as my ancestors did, for which the tickets were much less expensive, were brought on small barges to Ellis Island. When they landed, immigrants had to go through several tests before being allowed into the country. First there was the medical test. A medical examiner looked at each passenger for signs of disease. Those checking were especially concerned about an eye infection called trachoma, which was widespread in Europe but very rare in the United States. Trachoma is extremely contagious and can cause blindness and sometimes even death. Some people were prevented from leaving Europe because of an eye infection; others were forbidden to enter the United States because of it.

SADIE GRINGRASS, AUNT PHYLLIS'S MOTHER AND THE "REAL" GITTEL, AT AGE NINETEEN IN 1917. PHOTO COURTESY OF PHYLLIS RUBIN.

After the medical examination, immigrants were given a legal test. They were asked many questions such as "Are you married or single?" "How much money do you have?" "Have you ever committed a crime?" "Do you have a job waiting for you?" Immigrants who answered these questions to an inspector's satisfaction were allowed to enter America. Immigrants who did not answer these questions in a satisfactory manner were detained. About one in five immigrants who arrived at Ellis Island were detained for further medical or legal examination, but of those people, only two out of every one hundred were denied entry into the United States.

It is estimated that between 1880 and 1924 three million Eastern European Jews came to the United States. Jewish people under the rule of Russian czars were forced to live in segregated villages called *shtetls*. Many *pogroms* took place, and many people were killed. By 1920, more than one-third of the Jewish population of the Russian Empire had left for the United States. Many famous Jewish people entered America through Ellis Island during this time, including the science fiction writer Isaac Asimov, the composer Irving Berlin, and the political activist Emma Goldman.

Ellis Island is now an immigration museum with many exhibits containing photographs, artifacts, oral histories, and other displays. The American Immigrant Wall of Honor is a permanent exhibit that lists the names of more than 700,000 immigrants who entered the United States through Ellis Island. Two of those names are Ruth and Louis Levin, my maternal grandmother and grandfather, whose names were added by my family as a tribute to their memory.

To this day, thousands of people, including many children traveling alone, immigrate to America each year in search of a better life and a safe place to call home.

THE BRASS CANDLESTICKS FROM THE OLD COUNTRY THAT GRANDMA RUTHIE BROUGHT TO AMERICA. PHOTO BY MARY VAZQUEZ.

GLOSSARY

A sheynem dank: Thank you.

Challah: the beautiful braided bread eaten on the Jewish Sabbath and other holidays.

Ikh heys Gittel: My name is Gittel. (Gittel is a Yiddish girl's name that means "good," and it is pronounced with a hard "G" as in "goat.")

Pogrom: an attack upon the Jewish people, often carried out by government officials in Eastern Europe under Russian rule.

Shabbos: the Jewish Sabbath.

Shah: Be quiet. (Can be said gently: "*Shhh*" or harshly: "Keep quiet!")

Shayneh maidel: pretty girl; a term of endearment.

Shtetl: a small Jewish village or town in Eastern Europe before World War II.

Vi heystu?: What is your name?

Zei gezunt: Be well (equivalent to "farewell").

BIBLIOGRAPHY

BOOKS

Freedman, Russell. *Immigrant Kids*. Puffin Books: New York, 1980.

Moreno, Barry. *Images of America: Children of Ellis Island*. Arcadia Publishing: Charleston, SC, 2005.

Werner, Emmy E. *Passages to America: Oral Histories of Child Immigrants from Ellis Island and Angel Island*. Potomac Books: Dulles, VA, 2009.

WEBSITES

www.libertyellisfoundation.org/ellis-island-history

www.loc.gov/teachers/classroommaterials/presentationsandactivities/presentations/immigration/polish.html

www.nps.gov/elis/index.htm

www.ohranger.com/ellis-island/immigration-journey

For Aunt Phyllis—
I love you to pieces!
—L.N.

For all children who
come to this country seeking
freedom and safety
—A.B.

Library of Congress Cataloging-in-Publication Data
Names: Newman, Lesléa, author. | Bates, Amy June, illustrator.
Title: Gittel's journey : an Ellis Island story / Lesléa Newman.
Description: New York: Abrams Books for Young Readers, 2019. | Loosely based on true stories told to the author by her grandmother and aunt about their voyage to America. | Summary: "Brings to life a not too distant history of immigration to Ellis Island. When it's time for nine-year-old Gittel and her mother to leave their homeland behind and go to America for the promise of a new life, a health inspection stops any chance of Gittel's mother joining her daughter on the voyage. Knowing she may never see her mother again, Gittel must find the courage within herself to leave her family behind"– Provided by publisher.
Identifiers: LCCN 2017044804 | ISBN 9781419727474 (hardcover, jacketed, picture)
Subjects: | CYAC: Emigration and immigration—Fiction. | Ellis Island Immigration Station (N.Y. and N.J.)—Fiction. | Separation (Psychology)—Fiction. | Jews—United States—Fiction.
Classification: LCC PZ7.N47988 Gi 2019 | DDC [E]—dc23

Text copyright © 2019 Lesléa Newman
Illustrations copyright © 2019 Amy June Bates
Book design by Pamela Notarantonio

Published in 2019 by Abrams Books for Young Readers, an imprint of ABRAMS. All rights reserved. No portion of this book may be reproduced, stored in a retrieval system, or transmitted in any form or by any means, mechanical, electronic, photocopying, recording, or otherwise, without written permission from the publisher.

Printed and bound in China
10 9 8 7 6 5 4 3 2 1

Abrams Books for Young Readers are available at special discounts when purchased in quantity for premiums and promotions as well as fundraising or educational use. Special editions can also be created to specification. For details, contact specialsales@abramsbooks.com or the address below.

ABRAMS The Art of Books
195 Broadway, New York, NY 10007
abramsbooks.com